my mom is trying to Ruin my Life

For my mom, Judy
—K. F.

For Peter
—D. G.

SIMON & SCHUSTER BOOKS
FOR YOUNG READERS
An imprint of Simon & Schuster
Children's Publishing Division
1230 Avenue of the Americas
New York, New York 10020
Text copyright © 2009 by Kate Feiffer
Illustrations copyright © 2009 by Diane Goode
All rights reserved, including the right of
reproduction in whole or in part in any form.
SIMON & SCHUSTER BOOKS FOR YOUNG READERS
is a trademark of Simon & Schuster, Inc.
Book design by Jessica Sonkin
The text for this book is set in Mrs. Eaves.
The illustrations for this book are rendered in watercolor.
Manufactured in China

10 9 8 7 6 5 4 3
Library of Congress Cataloging-in-Publication Data
Feiffer, Kate.
My mom is trying to ruin my life / Kate Feiffer ;
illustrated by Diane Goode. — 1st ed.
p. cm.
"A Paula Wiseman book."
Summary: A young girl describes all the ways in which her
mother and father conspire to ruin her life.
ISBN-13: 978-1-4169-4100-2 (hardcover : alk. paper)
ISBN-10: 1-4169-4100-2 (hardcover : alk. paper)
[1. Mothers and daughters—Fiction. 2. Fathers and daughters—
Fiction. 3. Humorous stories.] I. Goode, Diane, ill. II. Title.
PZ7.F33346My 2009
[E]—dc22
2007045351

MY MOM IS TRYING TO RUIN MY LIFE

Kate Feiffer * Illustrated by Diane Goode

A PAULA WISEMAN BOOK

Simon & Schuster Books for Young Readers * New York London Toronto Sydney

This is my mom.
Sure, she looks like
a nice mom.

She makes people smile.
She makes people clean.
She gives hungry people food.

She takes people where
they need to go, and
then she picks them up
and brings them home.

She makes people's
boo-boos stop hurting.

And she helps people fall asleep when they can't.

But if my mom is such a nice mom,
why is she trying to ruin my life?

Here are five ways that my mom is trying to ruin my life.

way #1

She kisses me in front of my friends. She doesn't just kiss the top of my head. That would be bad, but not so bad. My mom gives me kisses all over my face.

way #2

She stops by my school in the middle of the day, barges into my classroom, and says, "I thought Emma might be hot and would like to change into these shorts." Like I would ever change my clothes at school.

I don't think so.

way #3

She talks too loudly.

way #4

She never lets me eat any
food that I think is
good for me.

way #5

She worries about everything and never lets me do
anything fun because I might get hurt, which I won't.

I've decided it's time to stop my mother before she ruins the rest of my life.

So I've come up with a plan.

The first thing I'll do is sneak out of the house when my mom isn't looking. Then I'll get on my bike and pedal away as fast as I can.

But what if my mom calls for me and I don't answer? She'll figure out that I snuck out of the house and biked away, and she'll get in her car and catch up to me.

This plan won't work unless I sneak out of the house, get on my bike, pedal away as fast as I can, and then, when she catches up to me, keep pedaling until I pedal down a steep hill into a muddy hole. She'll drive down the steep hill into the muddy hole, and her car will get stuck.

Only, I'll be stuck too.

And the hill is so steep that I can't pedal
my bike up it anyway. So my mom will
have to get out of her car and push me on
my bike up the hill.

But then, when I'm safely at the top of the hill,
I'll start biking away as fast as I can.

My mom will run after me,
but I'll be pedaling so fast
that she won't be able to keep up with me.

So she'll stop and go to a police station and tell them that her child has biked away.

And they'll look at her and ask, "Is it because you were ruining her life?" And she'll say, **"NO."**

But they won't believe her, so they'll put her in jail—for trying to ruin my life.

And they'll tell her she gets to make one phone call. And she'll call my dad, who, by the way, is also trying to ruin my life, only he does it in different ways than my mother does.

This is how my dad is trying to ruin my life.

way #1

He makes me do my homework as soon as he gets home from work, no matter what else I'm in the middle of doing.

way #2

He makes me turn off my light at eight o'clock at night even if I'm not tired.

way #3

He makes me clean my room even though it's already clean.

So my dad will go to the police station to get my mother out of jail.

But the police sergeant will see that he's trying to ruin my life too, and they'll arrest him.

Then my mother and father will both
be in jail, and my life will be . . .

perfect.

EXCEPT . . .

I will have biked home, and it'll be time
for dinner and I'll be hungry, but there
will be no one there
to feed me.

Then it will be time to go to bed, and there
will be no one there to read me a story.

There will be no one there to give me a kiss good night. And there will be no one there to tell me to turn off my light. And if I go to bed and I can't sleep because my light is still on and I suddenly get thirsty, there will be no one there to bring me a glass of water.

And then, if I do fall asleep and I have a bad dream because I went to sleep hungry and without any stories and nothing to drink, there will be no one there to hug me and say, "It's just a dream."

And I will be scared.

Really

scared.

If my parents are both in jail,
my life will be ruined.

"Mom!
    Dad!"

"I love you!"